GOODNIGHT
Ganesha

Written by Nadia Salomon

Illustrated by Poonam Mistry

PHILOMEL

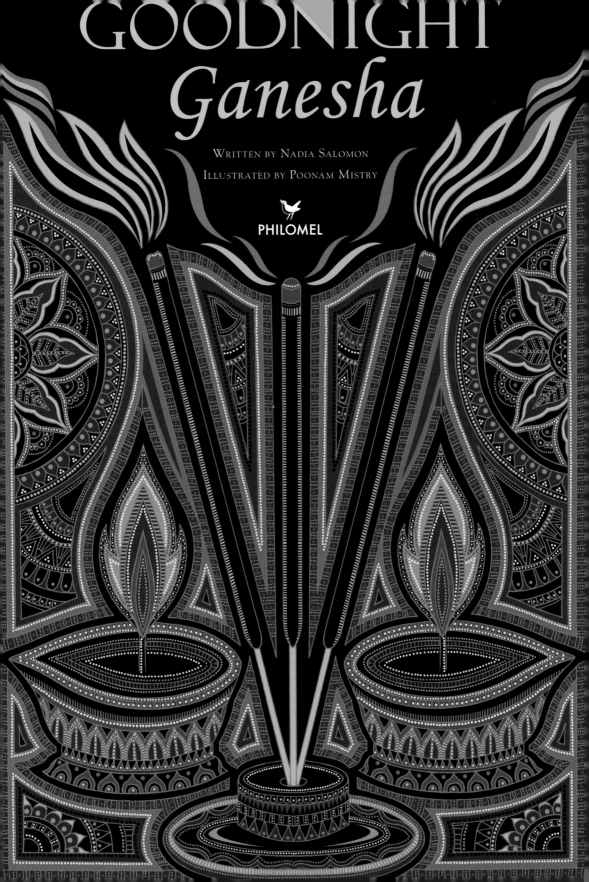

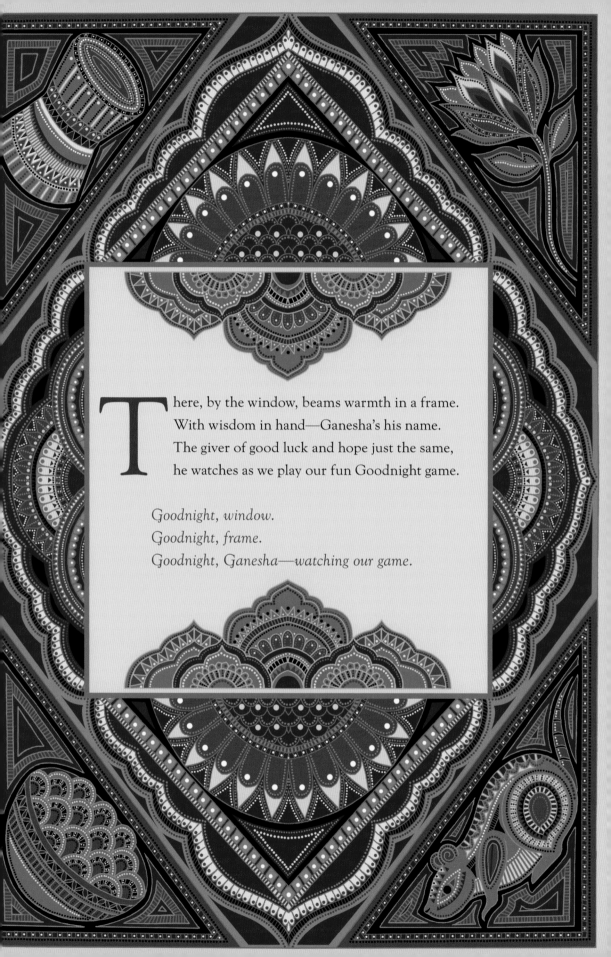

There, by the window, beams warmth in a frame.
With wisdom in hand—Ganesha's his name.
The giver of good luck and hope just the same,
he watches as we play our fun Goodnight game.

Goodnight, window.
Goodnight, frame.
Goodnight, Ganesha—watching our game.

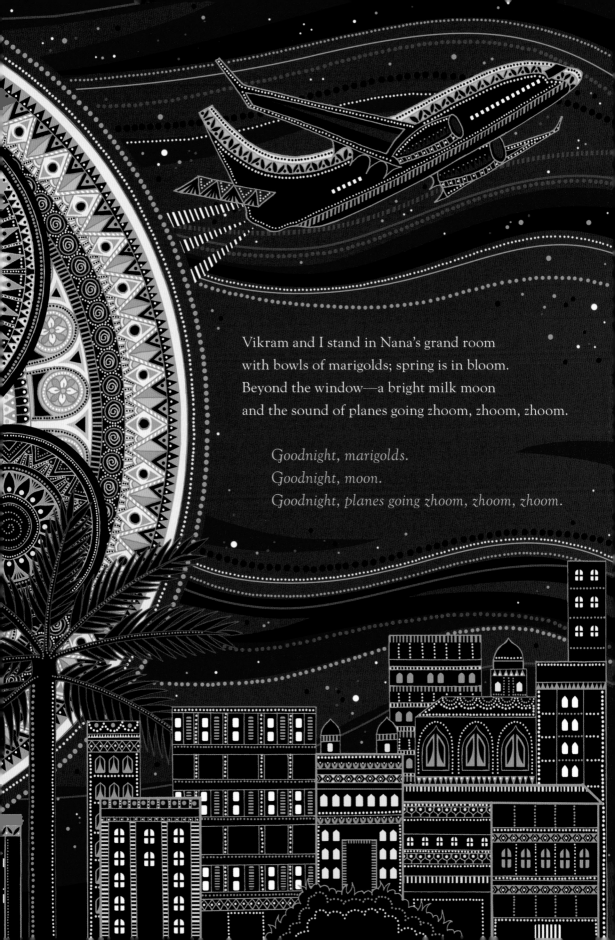

Vikram and I stand in Nana's grand room
with bowls of marigolds; spring is in bloom.
Beyond the window—a bright milk moon
and the sound of planes going zhoom, zhoom, zhoom.

Goodnight, marigolds.
Goodnight, moon.
Goodnight, planes going zhoom, zhoom, zhoom.

Nana leaves the curtains open but tied,
as a cool gentle breeze streams back inside.
I spin with the gust and look up, eyes wide—
a shy baby gecko scurries to hide.

Goodnight, curtains.
Goodnight, eyes wide.
Goodnight, gecko—"Peek-a-boo. Hide!"

BRAHMA

VISHNU

SHIVA

The marble mantle glistens with dew.
On it, three figures stand within view.
Golden idols, gleaming and new:
Brahma, Shiva, and Vishnu.

Goodnight, mantle.
Goodnight, dew.
Goodnight, Brahma, Shiva, Vishnu.

"You're it!" huffs Tata—face red as a beet.
"It's bedtime!" says Nana—voice raspy but sweet.
So we hustle upstairs to brush our teeth.
Tata kisses our hands, tickles our feet.

Goodnight, *tag.*
Goodnight, *teeth.*
Goodnight, *kisses and tickles on feet.*

While Tata tells stories from books we've read,
he kneads his pillow and burrows in bed.
Soon he grows tired and drifts off instead!
Then all is quiet—no words are said.

Goodnight, Tata.
Goodnight, bed.
Goodnight, pillow and words not said.

We fix a round tray—a thali, with kumkum.
Then gather together in the dim puja room.
We light a deepam—the air wafts with perfume.
Heads bowed, palms pressed—I smell flowers in bloom.

Goodnight, thali.
Goodnight, kumkum.
Goodnight, deepam—and wafts of perfume.

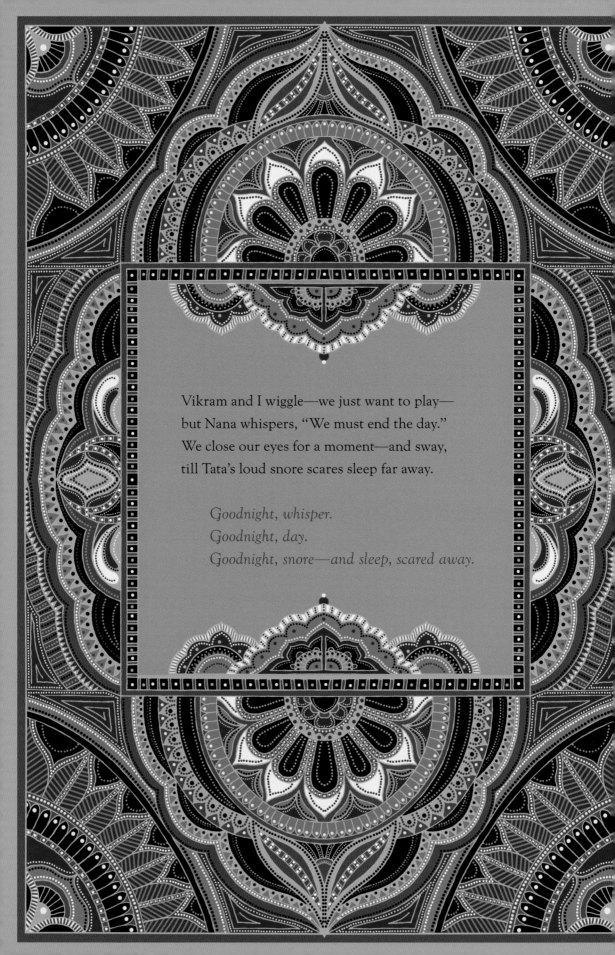

Vikram and I wiggle—we just want to play—
but Nana whispers, "We must end the day."
We close our eyes for a moment—and sway,
till Tata's loud snore scares sleep far away.

Goodnight, whisper.
Goodnight, day.
Goodnight, snore—and sleep, scared away.

We softly close the puja room door.
Then Vikram and I sit down on the floor,
ask Nana to spin just one tale more . . .
how the peacock stole the blue plumes it's known for.

Goodnight, *puja room.*
Goodnight, *floor.*
Goodnight, *peacock and what you're known for.*

Nana hums a serene lullaby
as she sips and savors her sweet, spicy chai.
Outside, a starry halo hangs high,
above the city and black night sky.

Goodnight, humming.
Goodnight, chai.
Goodnight, halo hanging high.

Sleep presses our eyes for a dreamy flight.
We stretch, we yawn, we hug Nana tight.
She reaches up gently to turn off the light,
while we lay down our heads and say goodnight.

Goodnight, sleep.
Goodnight, dreamy flight.
Goodnight, yawn—tired eyes welcome night.

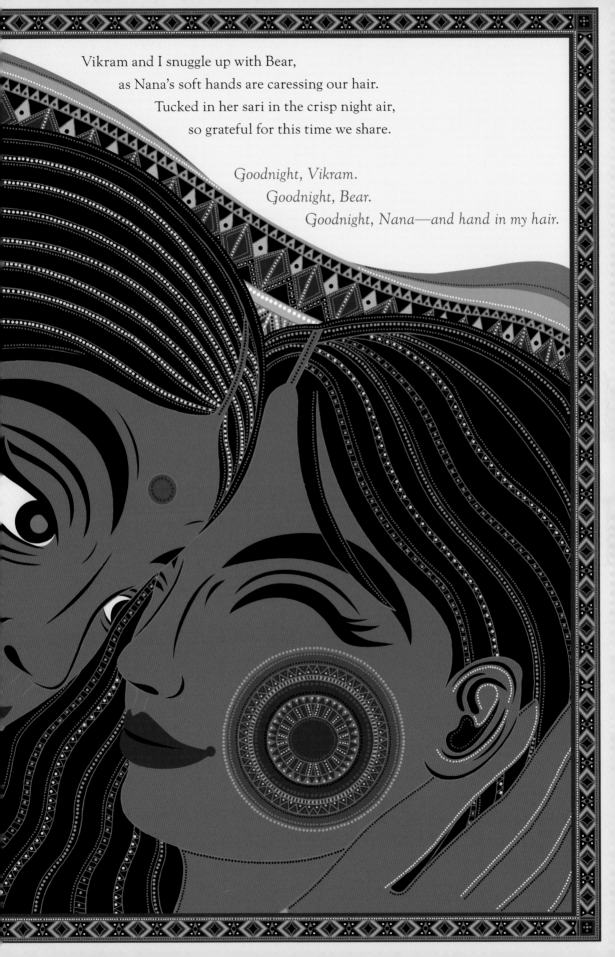

Vikram and I snuggle up with Bear,
as Nana's soft hands are caressing our hair.
Tucked in her sari in the crisp night air,
so grateful for this time we share.

Goodnight, Vikram.
Goodnight, Bear.
Goodnight, Nana—and hand in my hair.

And there, by the window, beams warmth in a frame.
With wisdom in hand, Ganesha's his name.
The giver of good luck and hope just the same,
he watches as slumber wins over our game.

Goodnight, window.
Goodnight, frame.
Goodnight, Ganesha—goodnight game.

Goodnight, *family*.
Goodnight, *love*.
Goodnight, *sweet Ganesha and stars up above.*

GLOSSARY

Brahma (Brah-ma)	Hindu god of creation
Chai (Cheye)	Hot black tea boiled with milk
Deepam (Dhee-pum)	Small oil lamp made of clay lit during puja ceremonies and on special occasions
Ganesha (Guh-nay-sha)	Hindu god of wisdom
Kumkum (Koom-koom)	Red powder made of turmeric used in puja ceremonies
Nana (Nah-nah)	Nickname for Nainamma (Grandmother)—father's mother in Telugu
Puja (Poo-jah)	Prayer, ceremony, blessing
Shiva (Shi-va)	Hindu God of Destruction
Tata (Tha-tha)	Grandfather (whether maternal or paternal) in Telugu
Thali (Tha-lee)	Ceremonial silver tray
Vikram (Vih-krum)	Boy's name
Vishnu (Vish-noo)	Hindu god of protection

AUTHOR'S NOTE

Nighttime routines hold so much nostalgia. No matter how different or similar our backgrounds may be, going to bed is a universal experience.

Whether it's taking a bath, having a warm drink, being read to, or being rocked to sleep, many people practice some kind of bedtime ritual.

As a child, I spent countless nights snuggled with my aunts or cousins, or burrowing under my ninen's (godmother's) tummy. Even now, as an adult, my own child and I have snuggled up together and shared Ninen's bed when visiting with her.

Goodnight, Ganesha is inspired by my own experiences, as well as those of my child visiting with a grandparent—in our case, Nainamma (Grandmother), in India.

I hope it inspires you to think about your own bedtime routines and traditions, and perhaps even create some new ones of your own!

Goodnight, Munchi.
Goodnight, family.
Goodnight, stars above.
Goodnight, goodnight—you are so loved.

Thank you for inspiring this dream . . .
—N. S. A.

For my family all over the world.
—P. M.

PHILOMEL BOOKS
An imprint of Penguin Random House LLC, New York

First published in the United States of America by Philomel Books,
an imprint of Penguin Random House LLC, 2021

Visit us online at penguinrandomhouse.com.

Library of Congress Cataloging-in-Publication Data is available.

Manufactured in China

ISBN 9780593203613

1 3 5 7 9 10 8 6 4 2

Edited by Liza Kaplan
Design by Ellice M. Lee
Text set in Goudy Old Style MT

The art was done in ink on paper and completed digitally.